GARCIA & Colette

GO EXPLORING

Hannah Barnaby
pictures by Andrew Joyner

G. P. Putnam's Sons

For Eamon and Lucy, my brave explorers —H.B.

For William and Charlotte —A.J.

G. P. PUTNAM'S SONS
an imprint of Penguin Random House LLC
375 Hudson Street
New York, NY 10014

Library of Congress Cataloging-in-Publication Data
Names: Barnaby, Hannah Rodgers, author. | Joyner, Andrew (Illustrator)
Title: Garcia and Colette go exploring / Hannah Barnaby ; illustrated by Andrew Joyner.
Description: New York : G. P. Putnam's Sons, [2017]
Summary: "Garcia and Colette can't agree about where to explore, so they set out on independent expeditions
before realizing that exploring is always more fun when your friend is by your side"—Provided by publisher.
Identifiers: LCCN 2016016731 | ISBN 9780399176753
Subjects: | CYAC: Friendship—Fiction.
Classification: LCC PZ7.B253 Gar 2017 | DDC [E]—dc23
LC record available at https://lccn.loc.gov/2016016731

Manufactured in China by RR Donnelley Asia Printing Solutions Ltd.
ISBN 9780399176753
1 3 5 7 9 10 8 6 4 2

Design by Ryan Thomann and Eileen Savage.
Text set in ITC Usherwood Std.
The artwork for this book began as brush and ink line on watercolor paper.
Then the drawings were combined, layered, and colored digitally.

GARCIA and Colette were
having a disagreement.

"Space!"
said Garcia.

"Sea!"
said Colette.

"Stars!"
said Garcia.

"Sand!"
said Colette.

There was only one thing to do.

"I will build a rocket," said Garcia.

"I will build a submarine," said Colette.

And at the same time, they said,
"I will go exploring."

They gathered their materials and got to work.

Garcia's rocket was snazzy and silver,
made of metal and bolts, with a
round window on the side.

Colette's submarine was gold and
glorious, made of metal and bolts,
with a square window in the front.

"Nice work," Garcia said.

"You too," Colette replied.

They prepared for their journeys.

Garcia packed fourteen peanut butter
sandwiches, a notebook, a pen,
and his lucky hat.

Colette packed fifteen peanut butter
sandwiches, a notebook, a pen,
and her lucky socks.

They were ready to go.

"Bon voyage," called Colette
as she climbed down her hatch.

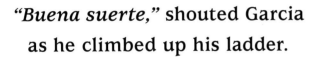

"Buena suerte," shouted Garcia
as he climbed up his ladder.

They waved to each other
through their windows.

The countdown began:

Colette watched Garcia's rocket lift
quickly into the sky. *Showy,* she thought.
But the blue flames trailing behind it
were quite beautiful.

Garcia watched Colette's submarine
glide quietly under the water. *So slow,*
he thought. But the sun shining on the
gold paint was mesmerizing.

Garcia's rocket
climbed up, up, up.
The sunlight thinned and
disappeared until the air
was like ink all around him.
He took out his notebook.
"Space is dark," he wrote.

Colette's submarine
sank down, down, down.
The water turned from
blue to navy to black.
She took out her notebook.
"The sea is dark," she wrote.

Garcia passed the moon.
He looked out his round window
and observed stars and meteors
and many glowing things.
"Space is beautiful," he wrote.

Colette floated over a coral reef.
She looked out her square window
and noticed exotic fish and other
creatures glowing like lanterns.
"The sea is beautiful," she wrote.

Garcia ate a peanut butter sandwich. All he could hear was
the sound of his own chewing, and then the scratching of
his pen as he wrote, "Space is quiet."

Colette ate two peanut butter sandwiches. She hummed a little eating song, as she often did, but her voice sounded louder than usual. "The sea is quiet," she wrote in her notebook.

Garcia began to wish he had made his
rocket a bit bigger inside. He wanted to
put on his lucky hat, but he couldn't
take off his space helmet. He wanted
to count the stars, but up close,
they were too bright to look at.

"Space is lonely,"
Garcia wrote.

Colette couldn't get comfortable. She wanted to put on her lucky socks, but she couldn't reach her feet. She wanted to put her toes in the sand, but she couldn't open the hatch underwater.

"The sea is lonely," Colette wrote.

Garcia took one last look at space.
Then he turned his rocket around
and started back down.

Colette took one last look at the sea.
Then she turned her submarine
around and started back up.

Garcia's rocket splashed down just as Colette's submarine popped up. They waved to each other through their windows. Colette towed Garcia back to shore.

"The sea was great," she told him. "But too much water."

"Space was awesome," Garcia said.
"But not enough air."

"I have an idea,"
said Colette.

It was nighttime when they arrived.

There was sand beneath their feet. There were
stars above their heads. There was darkness
and quiet all around them.

"Desert," they said together.

And they were not lonely.
Not one little bit.